# What Shall We Do When We All Go Out?

## A Traditional Song, Illustrated by
## Shari Halpern

**North-South Books**

*New York / London*

*FOR JUDY SUE*

*Text adapted by Philip H. Bailey*

*Published in the United States by North-South Books Inc., New York.*
*Published simultaneously in Great Britain, Canada, Australia, and*
*New Zealand in 1995 by North-South Books, an imprint of*
*Nord-Süd Verlag AG, Gossau Zürich, Switzerland.*
*First paperback edition published in 1997.*

*Library of Congress Cataloging-in-Publication Data*
*What shall we do when we all go ou? : a traditional song / illustrated*
*by Shari Halpern ; [text adapted by Philip H. Bailey].*
*Summary: Words and illustrations depict the activities of the day as children go out to play.*
*1. Children's songs—Texts. [1. Play—Songs and music. 2. Songs.] I. Bailey, Philip H. II. Title*
*PZ8.3H16Wh 1995 782.42'083—dc-20 [E] 94-38573*
*A CIP catalogue record for this book is available from The British Library.*

*The artwork consists of collages made with several different types of paper painted with*
*acrylics and watercolors, as well as color photocopies of pieces of fabric.*
*Typography by Marc Cheshire*
*The type is Laudatio.*

*ISBN 1-55858-424-2 (trade binding) 10 9 8 7 6 5 4 3 2 1*
*ISBN 1-55858-425-0 (library binding) 10 9 8 7 6 5 4 3 2 1*
*ISBN 1-55858-705-5 (paperback) 10 9 8 7 6 5 4 3 2 1*
*Printed in Belgium*

*For more information about our books, and the authors and artists*
*who create them, visit our web site: http://www.northsouth.com*

**What shall we do when we all go out,
all go out, all go out?**

**What shall we do when we all go out,
When we all go out to play?**

We will ride our three-wheel bikes,
three-wheel bikes, three-wheel bikes.
We will ride our three-wheel bikes
When we all go out to play!

**We will seesaw up and down,
up and down, up and down.
We will seesaw up and down
When we all go out to play!**

We will run and somersault,
somersault, somersault.
We will run and somersault
When we all go out to play!

We will wear our roller skates,
roller skates, roller skates.
We will wear our roller skates
When we all go out to play!

Then we'll sit and eat our lunch,
eat our lunch, eat our lunch.
Then we'll sit and eat our lunch
In the middle of the day!

*What shall we do in the afternoon,*
*afternoon, afternoon?*
*What shall we do in the afternoon*
*After we've had lunch?*

**We will stop to feed the ducks,
feed the ducks, feed the ducks.
We will stop to feed the ducks
After we've had lunch!**

**We will fly our long-tailed kites,
long-tailed kites, long-tailed kites.
We will fly our long-tailed kites
After we've had lunch!**

We will climb a great big tree,
a great big tree, a great big tree.
We will climb a great big tree
When we all go back to play!

We will all play hide-and-seek,
hide-and-seek, hide-and-seek.
We will all play hide-and-seek
till it's time for us to go!

What shall we do when we all go in,
all go in, all go in?
What shall we do when we all go in,
When we all go in from play?

We will sit and sip our soup,
sip our soup, sip our soup.
We will sit and sip our soup
And think about TOMORROW!

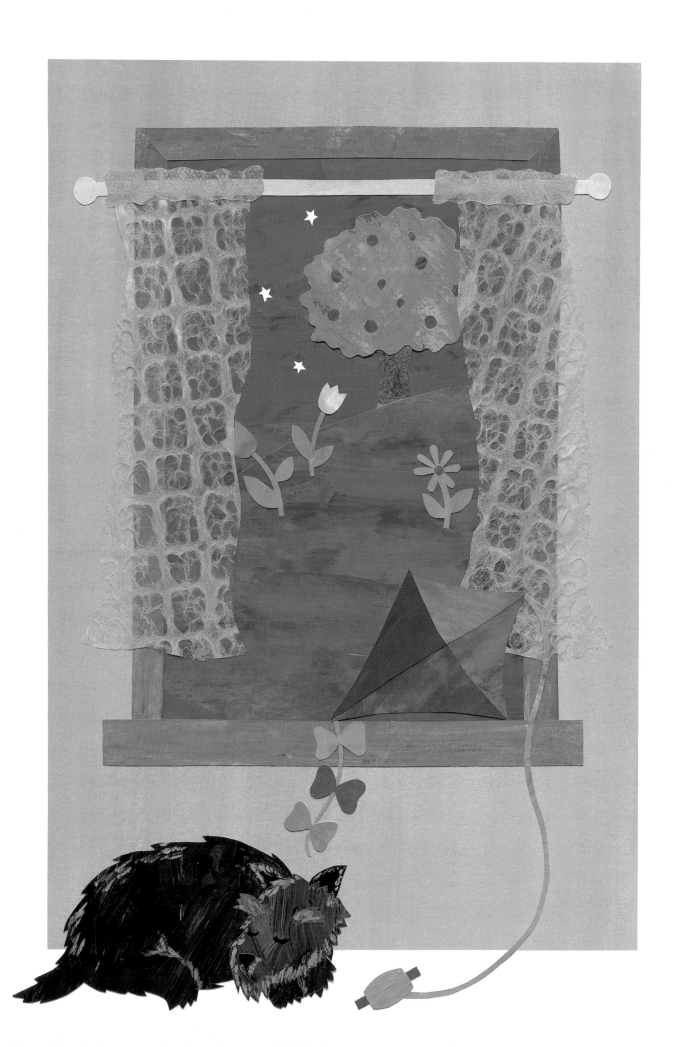